Dimity Duck

To Aaron, Brett, and Lexi, Hunter, Hayden, and Maya,
my newest grandnieces and grandnephews – J.Y.

Pour Lise – S.B.

First published in paperback in Great Britain by HarperCollins Children's Books in 2006

1 3 5 7 9 10 8 6 4 2
ISBN-13: 978-0-00-783797-7

HarperCollins Children's Books is a division of HarperCollins Publishers Ltd.

Text copyright © Jane Yolen 2006
Illustrations copyright © Sebastien Braun 2006

Visit our website at: www.harpercollinschildrensbooks.co.uk

Printed and bound in Malaysia

Dimity Duck

by Jane Yolen

illustrated by Sebastien Braun

HarperCollins *Children's Books*

Dimity Duck
waddles,
she **toddles**
out of bed.

Niddy-noddy
goes her tail
and *quack!*
goes her
head.

She brushes all
her feathers,
as gold as
new-mown
hay,

then smiles into
her mirror.

It's time to start
the day.

Dimity Duck
waddles,
she **toddles**
off to eat.

Wiggle-
waggle

goes her
tail

and p^{u}mp! go her feet.

She paddles off to breakfast. She dines on fish and weeds.

She finds
that
in the deep
blue pond
is all
the food
she
needs.

Dimity Duck waddles
she toddles
and she sings.

Giggle-gaggle
goes her
tail

and whoosh!

go her
wings.

Frumity Frog watches,

he splashes  in the pond.

He waves a foot at Dimity
of whom he's
very fond.

Dimity Duck waddles, she paddles to his side.

Splishy-splashy
go the two,
playing
seek-and-hide.

All day they play till Frog decides
to hide beneath a pad.

Dimity Duck
    can't find him,
and *sniff!*
    she's feeling
            sad.

Surprise!

Dimity Duck
waddles,

 she dawdles

and she dips.

She showers her
friend, Frumity,
with frithy-frothy
drips.

Frumity Frog
giggles,
he
wriggles
with
delight.

He
bubbles
and he
babbles
but – it's
getting on
towards
night.

Dimity Duck waddles,
she toddles
and grows
pale,

drifty-drafty goes
her head
and droop!
goes her tail.

She throws
her friend
big kisses
as the sun sinks
out of sight.

For Dimity
and
Frumity,
playtime
ends
with night.

Dimity Duck
waddles,
she gets
into her
gown.

She makes
her bed
and
plumps her
pillows
full of
eiderdown.

Dimity Duck
waddles,

she toddles
off to bed.

Sleepy-sloppy goes her tail...

...and snore goes her head.

Good night, Dimity.

Shhhhhhhhhhhh!